HOW BIG IS
GOD?

For Liv, Emma, and Jack—
May you one day know just how BIG your God really is!
Love, Mama
—L.T.B.

To the Mathias-Baker Volunteer Fire Company & Rescue
Squad, and to the generous spirit of
volunteers everywhere.
—L.J.B.

How Big Is God?
Text copyright © 2008 by Lisa Tawn Bergren
Illustrations copyright © 2008 by Laura J. Bryant

Printed in the United States of America.
All rights reserved. No part of this book may be used or reproduced in any manner whatsoever
without written permission except in the case of brief quotations embodied in critical articles and reviews.
For information address HarperCollins Children's Books, a division of HarperCollins Publishers,
1350 Avenue of the Americas, New York, NY 10019.
www.harpercollinschildrens.com
Library of Congress Cataloging-in-Publication Data is available.
ISBN-10: 0-06-113174-1 (trade bdg.) — ISBN-13: 978-0-06-113174-5 (trade bdg.)
Typography by Jeanne L. Hogle
3 4 5 6 7 8 9 10
❖
First Edition

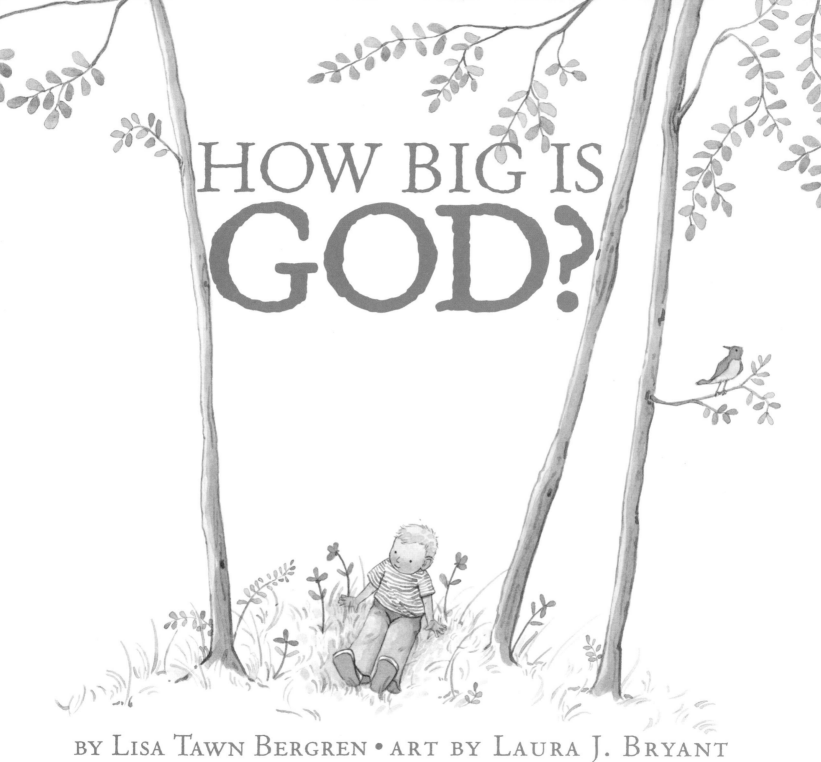

HOW BIG IS GOD?

BY LISA TAWN BERGREN • ART BY LAURA J. BRYANT

HARPER BLESSINGS

HarperCollins*Publishers*

"Mom, where does God live?"

"Why, he lives in your heart!" his mother replied.

The boy thought about that for a moment.

"If God is in my heart, he must be very, very tiny."

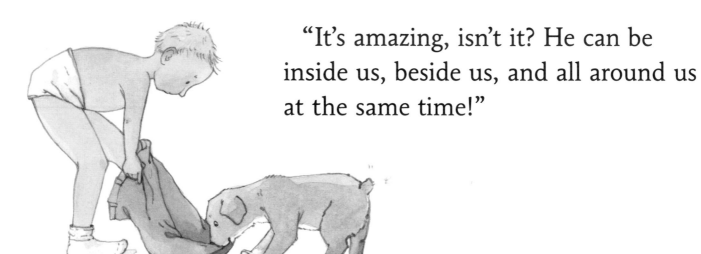

"It's amazing, isn't it? He can be inside us, beside us, and all around us at the same time!"

"If he's here with us, is he at our neighbor's house, too?"

"He can go anywhere he wants, all at once!"

"Like a *superhero*? Can he go through walls? Can he fly?"

"He doesn't have to fly. He's already there! He's everywhere. From Antarctica to the North Pole! From Argentina to Zimbabwe!"

The boy whispered, "But he's here? With us? Right now?"

"Right here, right now, *with us*," his mother whispered back.

"I don't get it."

His mother nodded. "You will.

He can be as tiny as a tree seed.

But what would that turn into?"

"The tallest

tree!"

"He can be as small as a snowflake
or as large as snowfields covering
those mountains! All at once!"

"He can be as small as a single drop of rain or as deep as the deepest ocean."

"Is he with my friends?" asked the boy.

"Of course." His mother lowered her voice. "And he's even with mean kids. They just don't see him!"

"Is he invisible?"
"At times. But God's everywhere
around us, if we train our eyes to see."

"He's like the wind. The same wind that can fly a kite also rushes over the peak of a . . ."

"Mountain!"

"That's right!"

"Can he be at school?"
"Your school, your friend's school, *every* school!"
"Even when I go on the bus?"
"With you on the bus, when you play on the playground, even when you take tests!"

"Can he reach the moon?"
"The moon, the stars, everything.
He can HOLD the whole universe in
his hands!"

"But Mom, how can he fit in so many places? And still be so small?"

"Think of him like sand, small enough to make its way into your sock. Or big enough to make a whole dune. A whole desert!"

"He's like the water, bubbling quietly
in a mountain spring, but becoming
a mighty . . ."

"WATERFALL!"

"That's right!"

"He's enormous, mammoth, gargantuan!"
"But eensy, weensy, tiny, too?"
"Yes! You've got it now!"

The boy sighed, tired after their long day together.
"I'm glad that such a big God can still fit in my heart, Mom."

"Me too. Out of all the places God is, that's his favorite place to be."